THIS BOOK BELONGS TO

_____

SUSPICIOUS

HAPPY

SCARED

SLY

WICKED

WORRIED

HUNGRY

NERVOUS

EXCITED

CUNNING

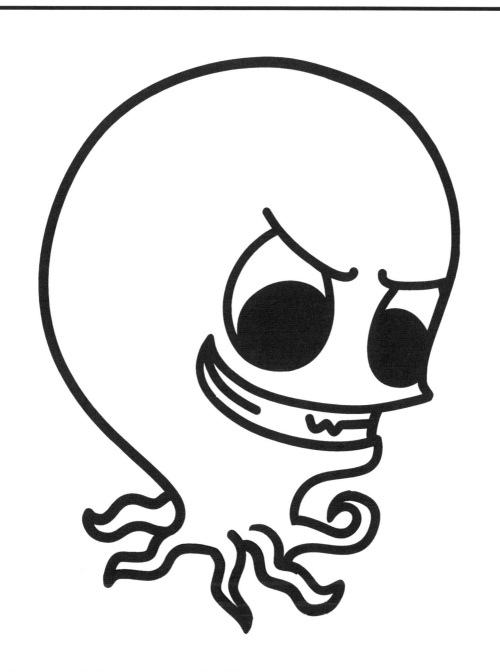

HAPPY

UNSURE

TIRED

SHOCKED

AFRAID

MAD

ANXIOUS

PLAYFUL

UPSET

AWKWARD

HAPPY

UPSET

SHOCKED

SAD

WORRIED

ANNOYED

SLEEPY

AMAZED

LOVED

Great Job!
YOU DID IT!

Made in United States
Troutdale, OR
06/01/2024

20250993R00018